O9-AIC-251

DreamWorks
HOW TO TRAIN YOUR
DRAGON

DreamWorks
PRESS
Los Angeles • New York

Especially for Miles and Mason

Written by Devra Newberger Speregen ★ Illustrated by Denise Shimabukuro and Shawn Finley
How To Train Your Dragon (A Pocket Full of Dreams) © 2015 DreamWorks Animation Publishing, LLC
How To Train Your Dragon © 2015 DreamWorks Animation, LLC
All rights reserved. No part of this book may be reproduced or transmitted in any form without written permission from the publisher.
Published by DreamWorks Press, 1000 Flower Street, Glendale, California 91201. ★ First Edition ★ Printed in the United States of America
2 4 6 8 10 9 7 5 3 1
12102014-D-2 ★ ISBN 978-1-941341-03-2 ★ Library of Congress Control Number: 2014949281
Visit dreamworkspress.com

Long ago, on a faraway island, fire-breathing dragons swooped down into the bustling village of Berk to steal food from the Vikings. And every night the Vikings tried to stop them.

But one Viking boy known as Hiccup was not allowed to fight dragons. Instead, his father put him to work in the village blacksmith shop.

Hiccup's father, Stoick, was the fearless leader of the Vikings. Hiccup begged his father to let him fight dragons alongside other kids.

But Stoick always said no. "You're too kindhearted and gentle to fight," he replied.

Now, Hiccup believed that if he could fight a dragon on his own, everybody would see that he was brave and strong.

One night, Hiccup made up his mind. He would sneak out and fight the dragons by himself!

Taking the Mangler—his new dragon-catching invention—Hiccup sneaked out of the shop. He found a spot outside the village, high up on a cliff, where he waited.

Suddenly, something zoomed by Hiccup's head. He could not see if it was a Gronckle or a Zippleback—but whatever it was, it was FAST and FURIOUS! Hiccup aimed the Mangler and fired into the darkness. Then he heard a loud ROOOAAAARRRR!

Hiccup's eyes grew big. "I think I got him!" he cried.

But there was no time to celebrate. Another dragon started chasing Hiccup through the village! Just before the dragon could get him, Stoick appeared and chased it away. Unfortunately, Hiccup had let all the other dragons accidentally get away, too. His father was furious.

A Viking boy pointed at Hiccup and laughed. "I've never seen anyone mess up so badly!"

The next day, Hiccup found the dragon caught in his Mangler's net.

"Wow," Hiccup said. "I really did it! And it's a Night Fury!"

Then he saw that the dragon's tale was broken. It was all his fault! Hiccup felt so bad that he cut the poor dragon loose.

The mighty beast leaped up and knocked Hiccup to the ground! Hiccup was really scared, but the dragon just turned and ran away.

At home, Hiccup thought about the Night Fury. He wondered why the dragon had not hurt him. Maybe all the bad things he had heard about dragons were not true.

Hiccup went to tell his father that he did not want to fight anymore. Unfortunately, it was too late. "You are going to the Dragon Training Academy," Stoick said.

Dragon Training Academy was a disaster. Astrid, a brave Viking girl, and the other kids made fun of Hiccup when he ran away from a Gronckle.

Gobber, their teacher, had to step in and save him. That made the kids laugh even more.

Hiccup could not stop thinking about the Night Fury.
He secretly built it a new tail fin. When Hiccup finally
found the crippled dragon, he knew it would not be easy
fitting it with the new fin. But Hiccup was gentle, and the
dragon began to trust him. He climbed onto the dragon's
back to test his handiwork.

"I did it!" Hiccup cheered as they flew through the sky.

Slowly the two enemies became friends. Hiccup named
the dragon Toothless.

Hiccup learned all sorts of dragon secrets from Toothless. He learned that dragons are ticklish and that they *really* hate eels!

Once at the Dragon Training Academy, Hiccup calmed an angry, two-headed Zippleback! Nobody saw Hiccup show the creature a yucky, stinky eel.

One day, a curious Astrid followed Hiccup after school.
"Don't be afraid," Hiccup told her. "Toothless won't hurt you."
They climbed onto the dragon's back and went for a ride.
Suddenly, there were more dragons in the sky.
Hiccup, Astrid, and Toothless followed them.
The dragons were taking the Vikings' food to their
leader, the Red Death!

When Stoick came to watch Hiccup's last battle, he thought his son was in danger. Stoick jumped in to battle the dragon himself. Just then, Toothless swooped into the ring and roared at the Viking chief.

Stoick charged toward Toothless.

"No!" Hiccup cried. "Leave him alone!" Hiccup explained that the dragons were being forced to steal food for the Red Death.

Hiccup pleaded with Stoick to free Toothless, but
Stoick would not listen. Hiccup went to the other kids.
"I need your help!" he told them. Then, he taught
them each how to ride the other dragons.

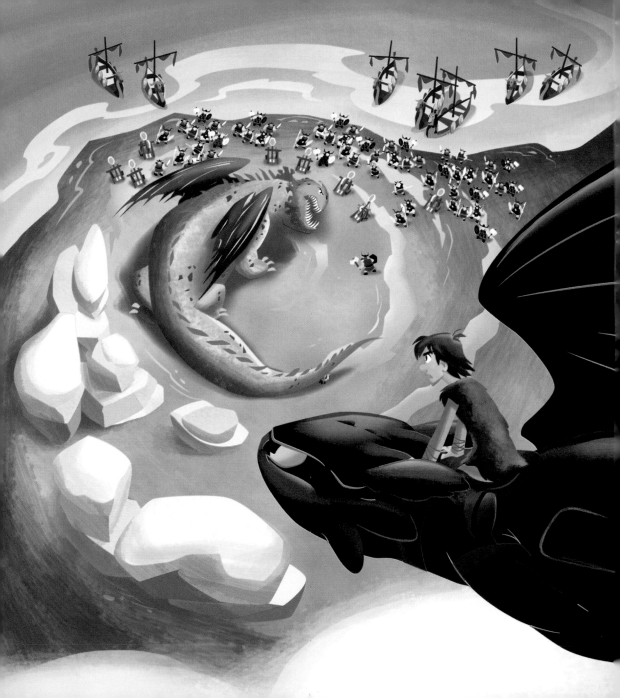

The Red Death was like no dragon the Vikings had ever seen before. He crushed their weapons and destroyed their ships.

Then something incredible happened. The Viking kids soared to the rescue!

Hiccup found Toothless and climbed onto his back. They flew very close to the enormous dragon's angry face.

The Red Death charged after Hiccup and Toothless.

Soon they found themselves in a perilous nosedive headed straight for the ground below!

At the last second, Hiccup and Toothless pulled away. But the giant dragon crashed into the ground at full speed!

Hiccup had tricked the terrible dragon. The Red Death was gone for good!

Although Hiccup was hurt in the fight, he was a hero. Now the Vikings *and* dragons loved him.

"I'm proud to call you my son," said Stoick.

Hiccup had saved the day and destroyed the worst dragon in the land. But best of all, he put the fighting between the Vikings of Berk and dragons to rest ... forever!

Before you close your sleepy eyes,
turn off the light for a surprise!

Sweet dreams!